# the sign fairy

Written and Illustrated by
Jill P. Harding

ISBN-13: 978-0-9964224-0-6

*Printed in the United States of America*

To
Michael Brown

and
Edward Michael Fanning

The images in <u>The Sign Fairy</u> are collages made up of pieces of paper, cards and photographs, that have been enhanced with colored pencil, ink and acrylic paint. Some of the paper I made by hand while in Walter Hamady's papermaking class at UW-Madison or with Gisela Moyer at Siever's on Washington Island. Other pieces were torn from magazines or purchased from scrapbook and mixed media resources. The photographs were taken by friends or myself and I used the internet and photocopies when appropriate.

Once the collage background was set, I'd paint and letter on top of it to create layers, depth and something of my own. These illustrations contain the words to a good thought and every page has at least one dragonfly and one heart incorporated in it. In total, there are 43 dragonflies and 43 hearts. Can you find them all?

I'd like to give credit to all the image makers in these collages, known and unknown, but especially to Cari Lewis, Mary Burns of Manitowish River Studio, John Atkinson Grimshaw, Tom Schroeder, Kathryn Brown, Google Maps and Michelle and Gary K of Chicago.

I want to thank Write On Door County and Nancy Carlson for the Writing and Illustrating Children's Books class. It planted seeds for this book. Mary Ellen Sisulak of Turtle Ridge Gallery and friend extraordinaire, encouraged those seeds to grow. Lou Ann McCutcheon's keen graphic sensibilities helped bring this book to fruition. And while I'm at it, I might as well thank all the friends and family who have helped me along the journey. Your belief in me, love and encouragement has made all the difference. Lastly, thank you to the souls who come and visit me at Good Thoughts. I hope I passed on the story you wanted me to tell.

Petra knew it was going to be a good day the minute she saw the big black crow out her window.

She lived in a place she loved,
far from the hustle and bustle,
on the north end of the
peninsula.

Her cottage was hidden from
sight, way back in a meadow
surrounded by trees.

She grew apples
and cherries
and pears.

Her garden was full of
tomatoes and sweet smelling
lavender.

There were rocks stacked in
towers and dragonflies and
hearts appeared everywhere.

Petra even had a heart shaped flower garden.

Eagles and owls often flew over it on their way from The Clearing to the rocky shores of the Headlands.

Everywhere she looked she saw beauty.

Her heart was full.

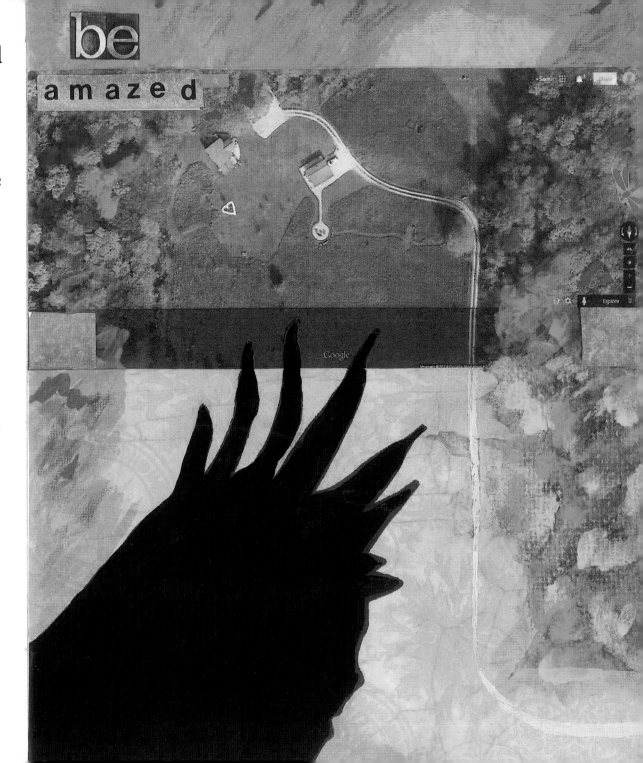

On warm days Petra liked to walk to the Ellison Bay Post Office and then stop for a glass of cider.

She would hike down the long gravel driveway that led out to the road going into town.

Petra thought that Garrett Bay was one of the prettiest roads in Door County as it meandered through fields and woods, and twisted along the water.

Sadly, not everyone saw the beauty or felt the peace that the road offered.

Some talked so loudly they couldn't hear the birds.

Some picked endangered flowers.

Others drove so fast they didn't see a thing... including Petra!

And a few left their garbage on the road.

walk

IN

beauty

Petra wanted to help others see the beauty around them and in each other.

She wondered how she could share her good thoughts and her full heart.

And just like that, she hatched a plan.

She recycled some boards from the old red barn that was falling down.

Then she measured, cut and carefully lettered...
before digging holes to put up a sign at the edge of the driveway down by the road.

YOU want TO SEE

The sign said 'good thoughts' on both sides so you could see it in both directions.

Attached to it and facing the road was another sign with a big red hook.

It said 'be'.

Some noticed the sign that
first day.

Petra hoped they were
thinking about good things...

like friends
or wild asparagus
or how lovely the white
birch trees looked against
the blue, blue sky.

The next day she hung a
small sign on the red hook
under the word 'be'.

It said 'kind'.

After that,
every day,
there was a new small sign
with another word.

It didn't take long before lots of people started going by the sign.

They thought about the words and sometimes remembered them later.

Cars went slower and some folks even stopped to take pictures.

A few of those pictures were printed in the newspaper and soon there was plenty of talk about the good thoughts sign.

People started calling Petra The Sign Fairy.

Petra was a private person.
She really didn't want to
be seen.

She just wanted her words
seen.

She liked being The Sign
Fairy, but she didn't think it
was important for people to
know about her.

What was important was
for people to take care of
each other
and the sky
and the food
and the water
and the roads
and the flowers
and the animals
and our beautiful planet.

Some mornings when Petra
woke up, she felt old and tired.

It felt like a struggle to
accomplish much of
anything at all.

But she knew she could do
one small thing.

She could think good
thoughts.

She could be The Sign Fairy.

# BEGIN AGAIN

be

patient

Thank you so much for your "good thoughts" each day. We have been staying down the road on Garrett Bay Rd the past 2 weeks and have been moved by your words each day as we've driven by.

Thank you again!

Thank you, sign fairy— for sewing seeds of good and reminding us of the important things. Bravo!

So what will you be?

You don't have to be big.
You don't have to be powerful.
You don't need talent
or loads of money.

You have to be kind.
You have to care.
Just be yourself.

And you must believe that
if everybody could do
one small good thing
every day, it would make
a big difference.

The world would be a better
place...

...and our hearts would be full.

be

GRATEFUL